Norman Bridwell
CLIFFORD'S®
FIRST SLEEPOVER

E
BRI

SCHOLASTIC INC.

New York   Toronto   London   Auckland   Sydney
Mexico City   New Delhi   Hong Kong   Buenos Aires

For Koto Coltrane Bridwell and her mother, Tsuyu
—N.B.

The author thanks Eva Moore and Manny Campana
for their contributions to this book.

ISBN 0-439-47285-7

Copyright © 2004 by Norman Bridwell.
All rights reserved. Published by Scholastic Inc.
SCHOLASTIC, CARTWHEEL BOOKS, and associated logos are trademarks and/or registered trademarks of Scholastic Inc.
CLIFFORD, CLIFFORD THE BIG RED DOG, and associated logos are trademarks and/or registered trademarks of Norman Bridwell.

Library of Congress Cataloging-in-Publication Data is available.

10 9 8 7 6 5 4 3 2   04 05 06 07 08

Printed in the U.S.A. • First printing, January 2004

Hi, I'm Emily Elizabeth. My dog, Clifford, and I are going to sleep over at Grandma's tonight.

The first time we slept over at Grandma's, Clifford was just
a tiny puppy. Mommy and Daddy were going to a party and
would not be back until late.

Mommy said I could take my doll. Clifford had to stay home.
He would be too much trouble for Grandma and Grandpa.

I gave Clifford some food and water. Mommy said
he would be all right until they got home.

I hated to leave my little puppy behind.

Mommy and Daddy drove me to Grandma's house.

Grandma and Grandpa were glad to see me.
So was Laddie, their dog.

I had my own room at Grandma's house. I left
my doll and suitcase there and ran downstairs.

Grandma made tomato sauce for our spaghetti dinner.
She had baked a blueberry pie just for me.

Before dinner we had to take
old Laddie for a walk.

Laddie was glad to get outside.

Laddie was a good jumper.

Laddie liked to roll in the grass.

Laddie loved to fetch sticks.

Grandpa had a little treat for Laddie.

Laddie gobbled it up.

Sometimes Laddie just liked to run.

We were getting hungry. It was time to go home and eat spaghetti.

We opened the door. What had happened?

What an awful mess. These tiny footprints could
only be made by one animal. . . .

I said, "Naughty puppy! How did you get here?"

It took us a while to clean up the mess.

I had to clean up Clifford, too.

We had a good dinner, but it wasn't spaghetti.

After dinner we watched my favorite programs.

Grandma called Mommy and Daddy and told them Clifford
was safe. She made Clifford a little bed of his own.

But Clifford had a better idea.

In the morning I said good-bye to Grandma and Grandpa.
It was a sleepover we would never forget.

Now when we sleep at Grandma's,
Clifford has his own room, too.